The Baldwins

THE BALDWINS

SERGE LAMOTHE

Translated by Fred A. Reed & David Homel

Talonbooks

Vancouver

Talonbooks
P.O. Box 2076, Vancouver, British Columbia, Canada V6B 3S3
www.talonbooks.com

Typeset in Adobe Garamond and printed and bound in Canada.

First Printing: 2006

The publisher gratefully acknowledges the financial support of the Canada
Council for the Arts; the Government of Canada through the Book Publishing
Industry Development Program; and the Province of British Columbia
through the British Columbia Arts Council for our publishing activities.

Les Baldwin by Serge Lamothe was first published in French in 2004 by Les
Éditions l'Instant même (Quebec). Financial support for this translation
provided by the Canada Council for the Arts and the Department of Canadian
Heritage through the Book Publishing Industry Development Program.

Library and Archives Canada Cataloguing in Publication

Lamothe, Serge, 1963–
[Baldwin. English]
    The Baldwins / Serge Lamothe ; translated by Fred A. Reed & David Homel.

Translation of: Les Baldwin.
ISBN 0-88922-544-3

    I. Reed, Fred A., 1939– II. Homel, David III. Title. IV. Title: Baldwin.
English.

PS8561.L665B3413 2006   C843'.54   C2006-901385-3

ISBN-10: 0-88922-544-3
ISBN-13: 978-0-88922-544-2

It is, after all, not necessary to fly right into the middle of the sun, but it is necessary to crawl to a clean little spot on Earth where the sun sometimes shines and one can warm oneself a little.

Franz Kafka
Letter to His Father

detectable through their isolation, their physical distress, or through indelible psychological traces.

It is regrettable (and condemned as such by Baldwinologists around the world as a point of honor) that the successes garnered in this specific field of research have given rise to a veritable spate of rumors, each more far-fetched than the other. Allow us to deplore such abuses. In our opinion, it would be perilous, not to say suicidal, to embark on a debate that could only aggravate the atmosphere of tension that already permeates the best-informed circles. In publishing this Report, the Institute hopes to put to rest any misunderstanding with regard to the question at hand: nothing, given the current state of research, allows us to conclude that the Baldwins are likely to rise once more to the peripheral surface of our conditioning.

It must be admitted, however, that since the election of the last government, basic research has suffered certain setbacks when compared to its bureaucratic derivatives. This is principally, and unsurprisingly, attributable to a pervasive loss of confidence in the doctrine of critical mass. Throughout these fifty years of behind-the-scenes efforts, while in many fields of scientific endeavor (particularly in medicine, not to mention astrophysics and communications) several veritable renaissances have occurred—while Batimur has brought us Perceptivism, while Murène has formulated his Peripheral Theory and while Feödik was carrying out his first series of differentiated manipulations—little has been heard about research into the Baldwins, per se. Perhaps that has been for the best. We nevertheless believe (as the present publication would tend to demonstrate, in eloquent confirmation of the accuracy of our prejudgements) that we are now ready to draw the appropriate lessons from Post-History.

Would basic research suffer were we to experience the urgent need to construct for ourselves an identity that would be neither artificial nor borrowed? Quite the contrary, it would seem to us; only now, as we are freeing ourselves from its grasp, has a thorough knowledge of the Baldwin cycle become essential.

< 8 >

Let us not deceive ourselves: no cyclopean expansion of civilizations peripheral to ours can be anticipated. The time has come to suggest coherent answers to certain questions.

To the first of these questions—the question that spontaneously occurs to the researcher and could be formulated thus: Do the Baldwins truly exist or are they a myth?—an ever-increasing number of Baldwinologists are tempted to answer, as did Kroutnen to his pupil, the immortal Sluger: "My dear fellow, of course the Baldwins exist; all this has been thoroughly demonstrated. The real question is this: Were you to meet one, could you recognize him?"

< 9 >

OLIVIER

His job was to tally the wild geese of Goose Lake, in the high tundra. He would spend months in that rock-strewn wilderness waiting, sitting atop a hummock created specially for that purpose. Notebook and pencil in hand, he would wait, as one season followed the other. In winter, the snow would gradually cover him until he totally disappeared. Only his eyes could be seen, for his attention never wavered while he was on duty and—even though the geese had never once come here in the depths of winter—he persevered, unshakeable, blinking only out of extreme necessity as he observed the lake that, it must be said, was more like a pond, though it may have been much larger at some indeterminate time.

In the spring, when the geese finally began to arrive, Olivier would get to his feet. His legs were nearly as stiff as a corpse's. He would shake off the ice that still partially encrusted him, and rub his hands together at length, in the following manner: with his two hands he formed a hollow into which he breathed short puffs. But to do that, he first had to set down his notebook and the stubby lead pencil on top of a flat, lichen-covered rock. As he gave himself over to his spring ritual, he kept a constant eye on the tools of his trade, in case a sudden gust of wind or a wild animal might carry them away. He would exhale warm breath between his hands and rub his numb fingers together, after which he would pick up his notebook and pencil. Only then would he return to his work. Which meant drawing a line in his notebook every time a new goose touched down noisily on the lake. The lines he drew were elegant, quite evocative of the great birds in flight.

Each year, however, fewer and fewer geese would stop off at Goose Lake, and each year the volume of Olivier's work slowly diminished. You might think he would be happy to see his task lightened, but that was not the case. He dreaded the day when, inevitably, he would find himself without a job.

Come evening, he would return home to his wife and children in their suburban dwelling at 47 Monk Street. He could recognize the place from a distance. His wife would be waiting for him amid the smells of cabbage soup and onion skins. His children would be playing in their rooms with their laser pistols, and he recognized them, too. Everything seemed familiar: the clothes he wore, the armchair in which he would sit to watch the evening news. He considered himself a happy man. His wife was young and beautiful, her skin the color of copper, her stomach flat, her breasts like tiny figs. But soon it would be morning.

There was no choice but to work. And the seasons were growing longer. No one had foreseen such a possibility. The winter wasn't growing longer than before as summer became shorter. Not at all. All the seasons were lengthening in disturbing, chaotic ways.

Our files show that, until quite recently, Olivier Baldwin's reports were received and duly registered. But the pages of his last notebook are blank. Some researchers believe that this unusual turn of events can be interpreted in only two possible ways. Perhaps—and this may be the most credible hypothesis— not a single goose succeeded in making the trip to Goose Lake that year and Baldwin, judging it unnecessary to comment on the situation, simply returned an empty notebook. Or perhaps Baldwin didn't know how to read or write, and no one will ever really know what happened at Goose Lake that year, nor what happened to Olivier himself.

< 12 >

Ruth

To access her dream, Ruth just had to blink. Once. Twice. That was all. She no longer saw the grimy, dust-covered factories, the abandoned warehouses, the dark sky shot through with flickers of sickly, distressing light. She no longer heard the hollow thump of incoming shells in the distance, nor the occasional lowing of beasts or of other things. She no longer felt the damp cold that weighed upon her breast, and tinged her cheeks with the pallor of death. Her heart had almost stopped beating. Not a breath of air entered her lungs. Her mouth hung open. She no longer saw the passing caravans, the disgusting beggars who slept in the swamps and fed themselves on God knows what. She no longer saw, heard or felt any of that. What she saw, only she could have said.

One thing is sure. From that day on, not one of the good intentions Ruth Baldwin displayed in the past ever appeared again.

TAKASHI

The wreck of a vehicle that had been Takashi's home since birth was no thing of beauty. He couldn't have said if it had been a garbage truck, a pick-up or an aircraft fuselage. He never formulated any such hypotheses. Its bulkheads were pierced with countless holes, its metal frame was rusted through, and this decomposing mass was his residence. Someone, it seems, had abandoned the vehicle in the heart of the Altiplano, and the original passengers must have continued their journey on foot. But even that explanation appears suspect. There had never been a road through this place, nor any trace of the direction they might have taken. Everywhere, as far as the eye could see, stretched the cordillera of the Andes. Perhaps the metallic hulk had simply emerged one day from the rock. It certainly did seem to be trapped in its stony grip. A skeletal, centuries-old tree had grown up in the middle of the shelter. Takashi husbanded it with care, just as he watched over the nuclear cell that provided him with heat and light.

The civil servant's life suited him perfectly. Takashi had always had a gift for administrative tasks. His work pleased him, but took much of his time, and Takashi found himself dreaming more and more often of a leave of absence or a sabbatical.

That day, when Falstaff and Gudrun presented themselves to visit the apartment for rent, he found that he had forgotten the advertisement he had placed several decades earlier. The two men's appearance distressed him. Their clothing was in tatters, as if they had undergone a long and trying journey fraught with snares and unexpected perils. The air raids, ferocious beasts, bloodthirsty pirates and long stays in the camps must have been responsible for their derelict condition. But Takashi felt no need to speculate on that.

They exchanged rough greetings. Negotiations began immediately. They were complicated by the fact that Falstaff spoke a foreign language. Gudrun was actually no more than an interpreter hired at great cost, who turned out to be as incompetent in translation as in all other matters. In fact, Falstaff and he spoke quite distinct languages, neither of which bore any resemblance to Takashi's dialect.

Nonetheless, they visited the property. The apartment was not as spacious as the advertisement had led them to believe. It was a little less than one square meter wide, and one and one-half meters high, located between what had possibly been the driver's seat and the passengers' zone. The free and unlimited use of the energy produced by the nuclear cell represented its main attraction. Which was, as it happened, the first item to be negotiated. After having defined the space proposed in the advertisement—each had to huddle there in turn to experience the comfort, though Gudrun remained standing, and stretched out his arms as if to show that it was impossible for him to extend them completely, whereas Falstaff was happy to sit and close his eyes, upon which it seemed to Takashi that his contented smile expressed a lively interest in the apartment—Takashi demonstrated the cell's marvelous possibilities: he first used it to heat a small amount of water to prepare rock tea. His guests were extremely grateful. Their journey had been exhausting and the rock tea comforted them. Come nightfall, Takashi executed a dance that looked like a ritual or some form of invocation or other, then lit a lamp that shone a pallid glow on the walls of the fuselage. That was enough to convince Falstaff: here was a magnificent opportunity, staring him in the face. The months that followed were taken up with negotiations over the amount of rent.

Takashi fell badly behind in his work and complained of the added stress created by his visitors' presence. Day by day, however, each one better understood the other's language and the

< 15 >

negotiations progressed imperceptibly. It rapidly became clear that Gudrun would serve as currency. Falstaff had not simply hired his interpreter's services as Takashi originally thought: he had acquired him outright. This extravagant expense, added to the journey he had undertaken, had ruined him.

Takashi wanted nothing to do with Gudrun. To support his argument, he pointed out the lack of space. The apartment was far too confining for the two of them to stay there, and it was out of the question for Gudrun to share Takashi's lodgings in an even more reduced space. Several possible solutions were envisaged. Falstaff spoke in Gudrun's favor. He praised those facets of his personality that displayed him to best advantage. He almost succeeded in convincing Takashi as he described Gudrun's difficult childhood. In the end, having run out of ideas, Falstaff proposed that they cut down the tree, to which Takashi strenuously objected for sentimental reasons. He counterproposed that they feed off Gudrun during the long winter months, but Gudrun vetoed the proposition and, since his owner did not look kindly on that alternative either, the matter was dropped. History does not record whether Gudrun was eaten in the end, ingratitude being the daughter of necessity. But as certain chroniclers have correctly pointed out, once that critical phase of negotiations had ended, not the slightest allusion to Gudrun Baldwin can be found. Some believe that they had no choice, while others are of the opinion that the issue was resolved secretly, via signals transmitted surreptitiously between Takashi and Falstaff. While no one can confirm that the talks broke down over this particular issue, it is known that the nuclear cell stopped functioning several years later. Many have maintained that this unfortunate event contributed to hastening the departure of the would-be tenant. On one point the chroniclers are unanimous: Takashi Baldwin's apartment is still for rent.

< 16 >

BASMARA

My name is Basmara. I grew up in Amsterdam at a time when that city could still boast of a population of fifteen inhabitants, all of sound mind and body. Of course, the law required that the fifteenth citizen leave the city and, of course, I was that citizen. But that's another story: my own. And since I don't want people to think that the only story I know how to tell is my own, I've decided instead to tell how Magali and Richard met.

It happened on December 17 of that same year, somewhere between Saint-Viatique and Buenos Aires. All the versions of the story agree on that point, though they do diverge on others. So I will stick to the version that Natasha Baldwin used to sing to me when I was still a stubborn, imploring young nanny goat.

The important thing to remember is that the meeting might never have taken place. Magali had been traveling northward on foot for several months, while Richard had been making his way south. Both of them had, on the very same day, left their birthplaces to let themselves be guided by an inner voice that from time immemorial had been urging them to take to the road, promising them an ineffable, almost unspeakable happiness: that, perhaps, of finding themselves in the arms of a being of such cruel likeness to and yet so deliciously different from themselves. Once on the road, the inner voice had faded, and they finally stopped attending to it at all. For months, for years, they walked without encountering a living soul, and they began to suspect that the voice was a source of false hopes. Then on December 17, at around two o'clock in the afternoon, Richard stopped beneath a sycamore tree for a short rest. He may have fallen asleep for a moment. He raised his head just in time to see Magali's frail silhouette against the horizon. Suddenly, Magali caught sight of the man getting to his feet beneath the sycamore, as though he had emerged from the earth itself, and watched as he slowly raised his right hand above his head. The gesture struck her as being out of the ordinary. It was neither a distress signal nor a form of salutation. In the deliberateness with which the man raised his right arm, Magali could almost glimpse the summum of happiness, experience, acrobatics and audacity that fifty or sixty years of life together with that man might bring. The education of a child, perhaps even of a second one with the benediction of the elders—all that passed for a moment before her tired eyes. She raised her left arm, but her gesture was by no means a response. She did not wave it, but simply spread her fingers, a way of indicating her presence and her agreement not to flee. Richard interpreted the event in his own way. For him, it was as if he and the woman belonged to one another, body and soul. He would savor the centuries of shared existence and the rewards of a lifetime of toil, on the fishing boats or in the mines, dedicated to the well-being and security of his own. Richard Baldwin, who had never touched a drop of alcohol, stumbled like a drunkard beneath the weight of his revelation.

Night fell and the couple remained as they were, separated by several hundred meters, arms and hands upraised. Then came the darkness of twilight; they could make out no more than the improbable vibration of the other. When the moon rose, at last they could see their reflections in each other's eyes, freeing themselves from an eternity of spiteful frustration and superfluous deprivation. The sense of wonder each inspired in the other gave every indication of lasting. So spoke their inner voice and, this time, they listened to it.

On February 17, Magali began to lower her arm. Richard did the same on March 17 of that same year. The following day, they began walking once more.

< 18 >

Some estimate the probability of Magali and Richard meeting again at one in one hundred billion or more, and that is why the chroniclers perpetuate the memory of that single encounter. That is all that Natasha Baldwin, I and the others have to say.

< 19 >

BEN

Ben had his consultant's office only a few kilometers from the northwest exit of the secondary corridor. No one knew where he'd gotten his knowledge of the sciences of the old-time healers. He claimed that one of his ancestors had come to him in a dream to whisper instructions into his ear, describing the exact procedures to be followed for curing this illness or that, but none of that explained anything, said the sceptics. "If Ben gets his knowledge from his ancestor, just who did the elder get it from?"

That wasn't it at all. Most people in the know will tell you that Ben learned anatomy through the constant consultation of an old illustrated magazine that depicted young ladies harnessed in strange battle suits that did not cover too much of them.

He was surrounded by clouds of rumors. According to one, Ben was married to a scandalously rich Andalusian woman who paid for his medical studies in Norway and to whom he had promised, in return, to have a child by natural means (a promise that, no doubt for ethical reasons, Ben never kept). For most people—and it certainly wasn't the least damaging of the vicious rumors whispered behind the shaman's back—Ben was nothing but a charlatan who would gladly bill you a squirrel or even a pigeon for inflicting a simple abrasion that he would then do his best to infect, so you died of gangrene even before you had the chance to be sorry you'd spent your squirrel or pigeon.

But there's at least one case of healing, real or imaginary, if we are to believe prevailing opinion, attributable to the care provided by Ben Baldwin in his office on the secondary corridor. The event took place the same year the last government was elected.

A woman of a certain age (the chroniclers almost always omit her name, which they pretend not to know, even though some of them insist on calling her Natasha) appeared at Ben's office one toxic morning in April or June and asked that her bird of prey be examined on the spot. The bird may have been a bustard or a gyrfalcon. It was difficult to tell, and the woman was totally uncertain herself. In any event, a cursory examination revealed that the feathered creature was stuffed, and that this state of affairs was responsible for its rigidity.

"Can you fix it?" asked the woman. Ben hesitated to get formally involved. He first wanted to consult his illustrated magazine, but it was despairingly silent about everything that concerned, in any way, birds of prey, particularly stuffed ones. Still, Ben leafed through it for several hours. He didn't want to be defeated by the first obstacle, and he wanted to restore hope to the woman, who was now weeping on his shoulder and was likely, at any moment, to abandon her venture and take back the piece of broken glass she had offered as proof of her good will when she came into his office. A part of the original label remained glued to the curved glass fragment. Ben could make out the letters VE VE CLI.

To bring the bird back to life, some claim that the shaman used a rather unorthodox pomade made of blood, urine and topsoil. The recipe did not appear in the illustrated magazine, and Ben would later claim that one of his ancestors had telegraphed it to him the night before. The preparation took several years to prove its efficacy. Let us not lose hope, Ben repeated. The woman refused to abandon her bird. She moved into the closet next to the entrance. Every day at noon, during the quarter-hour of half-light that the sky provided, the woman emerged from the secondary corridor with her bird. She coated it with pomade, set it on its perch and encouraged it as best she could, with cries and gesticulations, to flap its wings and fly away. Finally, on October 17 of that year, it happened. The bird described several circles at

< 21 >

low altitude. Then it soared higher and higher, at an incredible elevation, before diving and vanishing in the direction of the Desert of Ziph.

Malicious gossip has it that even Ben Baldwin was surprised by the outcome. The same rumor-mongers claim that the healing of the bird should be attributed to the woman's care, and not the pomade Ben concocted. Even so, up to the present day, many people pay two or even three squirrels to purchase the tiniest quantity of pomade, which they leave to their children in the event they have children, or use on themselves as a last resort.

< 22 >

BEVINDA

Bevinda lived in a world where children could be held as slaves. Every day, they died by the thousands. She knew that. But it didn't stop her from drinking the Grands Crus Bourgeois of Bordeaux. It stopped nothing.

The war had ended long ago. Civilization, even longer ago. Humanity, no one could say exactly when. Scattered snipers concealed in the ruins survived against all common sense.

Bevinda lived in a world where the plague, leprosy and cholera raged a few blocks from her home. Still, she was enchanted by the miracles of fiber optics, and secretly hoped to soon be a recipient of stem cells as compatible as they were necessary. She would fall asleep in the evening, in front of her television set, long after the day's broadcasting was done:

> *All is well. Africa was put up for sale today. Spectacular views of the Indian Ocean. The international press has been taken hostage by prospective buyers, and barricades have been set up on most major thoroughfares to encourage foreign investment.*

The year the last government was elected, she lived alone in Zone C 24, some two hundred light years from herself, perhaps more. That was the least of the inconveniences with which she had to learn to live: that she lived alone, two hundred light years from herself in a world where children could be slaves—bought, sold, deposited in payment of balance owing or left as warranty.

All the television news was the same:

> *A bomb exploded in a school yesterday. A group calling itself* The Childhood Avengers *claimed responsibility.*

*Reprisals will be bloody. The army lashes out violently;
psychosis takes hold. The peace process will not be affected,
affirm the Presidents, praising it fulsomely.*

If Bevinda had said, "I cannot live in a world where such things are possible. My heart would stop beating. I would dissociate myself." Had she said that, she would already be dead.

But she kept on. She filled her glass and drank to the health of all the world's slaves, she fell asleep every evening and dreamed of nothing but captivity, vengeance and revolution. But she kept on.

Poor Bevinda.

< 24 >

Bruno

The world's smallest natural satellite is visible from the island of Borneo, on the Indonesian side of the former border, in the depths of the jungle some sixty kilometers north of the Mahakam River. The Dayaks named this minuscule moon *Dayak*. To reach the luxuriant valley that lies at the foot of Bukit Batubrok, at two thousand three hundred meters above sea level, the traveler must carry patience, as well as a machete. At the end of an exhausting expedition, having struggled on foot for endless weeks through remarkably dense tropical forests, he will be rewarded with a view of a natural wonder unlike any other. If the traveler has hired authentic Dayak guides and if he has, at the appropriate moment, taken the traditional oath of non-disclosure they insist upon, the Dayak will manifest itself to him in the form of a huge cigar measuring some forty meters long with a diameter of a bit less than eight meters. It will be floating in geostationary orbit, some four hundred meters above the valley of the Arüno.

Sure, of course. That's impossible.

Which is why nothing, absolutely nothing in the known universe can prepare travelers for the astonishing spectacle of the Dayak, and this is perhaps why most of them never return from an adventure that they soon consider to be a mystical illumination. Indeed, from the vantage point from which it is usually seen for the first time, the Dayak resembles a natural promontory more than a heavenly body. It is an optical illusion that some chroniclers are quick to describe as a metaphor for stubborn persistence. For it appears to have attached itself to the precipitous cliffs of Bukit Batubrok with the greatest possible unnatural obstinacy. At this stage, nothing can differentiate it from the other rock formations that seem to have been spewed out by the now dormant volcano.

The exhausted traveler now begins his first circumvolution. Given the natural barriers of the jungle and the Bukit Batubrok massif, this should last at least a week. Using shortcuts known only to themselves, Dayak guides may well be able to save a day or two, but superstitions and taboos have such force here that the guides will consciously slow the pace of the traveler's progress should he show too much haste. In seven days, the Dayak will have completed a full revolution—as will have the traveler, though in the opposite direction, meaning that he will find himself at the same spot he saw the Dayak for the first time. The difference is that, this time, he will be in a position to discover that the mysterious rock truly does float four hundred meters above the ground and is not joined to the jagged flanks of Bukit Batubrok. The chroniclers contradict one another on the subject of the second circumvolution. (They become totally incoherent when it comes to reporting the effects of subsequent circumvolutions.)

It has been claimed that the Dayak tree becomes visible only after the third and seventh circumvolutions. A risky assertion, bearing in mind that some travelers have accomplished as many as nine without ever having beheld that mythical tree of such extraordinary dimensions as to make the Dayak appear two or three times smaller than it is. Meaning that the age-old tree (which does not belong to any of the eight hundred varieties catalogued in the forests of Borneo) must have sent down such powerful roots into the extraterrestrial soil of the Dayak that it was long feared they would eventually cause the moon itself to break into fragments.

Around 1877, the moon of Borneo made headlines when a Baldwin from Kalimantan attempted to construct a walkway that would bridge the twenty-meter gap separating the Dayak from the rocky flanks of Bukit Batubrok. An article published in a local newspaper described the difficulties encountered by the project engineer. It would appear that because of the moon's rotation, the

< 26 >

idea of a retractable walkway had been rapidly abandoned and the engineer, a certain Victor Baldwin, dismissed without compensation.

Some Dayaks claim that their ancestors were past masters of the art of the *Dayak Leap*. This seasonal ritual consisted of spanning the twenty meters that separate the steep slopes of Bukit Batubrok from the tiny natural satellite in one enormous bound. But no Dayak has claimed to have performed it for so long that malicious gossip within the Dayak community itself is suggesting that the Dayak Leap may be nothing but a legend. Some have even accused an obscure employee of the Ministry of Tourism of being the author of such propaganda.

Were we to credit the contentions of Bruno Baldwin, the celebrated Peruvian contortionist, nothing would lead us to believe that the Dayak Leap is impossible. And so, next Friday evening, Bruno will be attempting the twenty-meter leap said to have been unspanned for thousands of years. Bruno Baldwin will perform his leap without a safety net, and he should succeed on his first effort without being seen. Observers warn that he is doomed to fail. This Friday, the Dayak will be visible only for a brief instant, at best a few nanoseconds, and Bruno runs the risk of being dashed to smithereens at the foot of Bukit Batubrok.

Then we will find out who has gotten the story right: the Dayaks, the Ministry of Tourism or the person who calls himself Bruno Baldwin, contortionist.

< 27 >

ENAYAT

Enayat had a son. A Baldwin. Did he find him by himself? No one could say. The child was an accidental and painful excrescence he alone had to bear, unaided. Long ago, someone might have called it a feeling, and even given it a name. No one made that kind of dramatic declaration any more. The certainties were so few. The pack ice was one with the sky; that was one of them. Another was that, as far as the eye could see, a fine dusting of ash covered that ice.

Enayat did his best to keep his son alive, administering as many as six or seven transfusions a day. Despite his efforts, the younger Baldwin was deteriorating, as was his father. The sight of these two Baldwins, father and son—holding hands, or steadying one another by the shoulders—was enough to melt the glaciers. Streams of fine grey ash flowed toward the sea and no one acknowledged their arrival.

From time to time, on its return migration, a humpback whale would leap from the water and throw a suspicious glance at the Baldwins. For a brief instant their cares grew lighter. Their solitude weighed no more heavily on them than on anyone else.

One day the son asked, "Father, when will we know that it's over?" And the father did not know what to say.

Perhaps ice was all that remained. Perhaps. There was no way of being sure.

With his tears, the father hydrated his son as best he could. But that wasn't enough. It hadn't been enough for some time. The whale could have helped them understand that. To give such knowledge was part of its duties and jurisdiction. But it felt neither the need to do so, nor even to mention it.

The whale swam back across the sea and forgot the Baldwins.

GREGOR

The sect had few members. Perhaps there was a time when they swarmed like insects across the face of the earth, but in the era of which I speak, only seven remained.

They were waiting.

For whom or what, they hardly knew. But they waited fervently, jammed one against the other in a malodorous grotto that they named, in a praiseworthy attempt at self-derision, *The Temple*. At the entrance to the Temple, rubbish and refuse accumulated, peculiar objects whose use the members of the sect no longer understood.

One of the seven—certain chroniclers attest that it was Gregor—took the initiative one day to send a message to the Universal House of Love, Justice, Prosperity and Peace. The majority of chroniclers agree that he would have used a fully mature red squirrel for that purpose. When at last the answer arrived, no one could remember what the question had been. The Universal House answered as follows: *Permission Granted.* That should have signified, whether in two words or ten thousand, that they had been authorized to undertake a pilgrimage to the Holy Land.

First obstacle: not one of the seven members of the sect knew where the Holy Land was, nor whether it still existed. The Temple and the area surrounding the grotto were immediately renamed *Holy Land,* and no one moved a muscle.

One day, the sect gave birth to a male child. They did not give him a name. Nor did they immolate him. They were happy just to let him cry. For which the little Baldwin displayed an inexhaustible talent.

When the child reached the desired degree of chubbiness, someone proposed that they eat him. At first, all the members of the sect seemed to accept the principle. But the key question, which was how to go about eating the infant without violating any taboos, touched off a sharp controversy. Schism loomed. Gregor proposed that they put it to a vote; his proposal was coolly received. Vote they did, ultimately, but the outcome only worsened the situation. Three members of the sect voted to roast him on a spit, three vaunted the advantages of raw meat and the seventh abstained. That left no room for interpretation. Which is why, in the end, they appealed once more to the supreme wisdom that emanated from the Universal House of Love, Justice, Prosperity and Peace. The answer took several years to reach them. It read: *Permission Granted.* So they devoured the troublemaker who had cast a blank ballot.

It never occurred to the members of the sect that they had exercised their democratic right.

The members of the sect are seven in number. No one knows how the law originated. Thus it has always been, and thus it will always be. As the years passed, these Baldwins accumulated so much refuse at the entrance to their grotto that they could no longer leave it. Messages from the Universal House of Love, Justice, Prosperity and Peace failed to reach them. Their own messages were lost at the Temple entrance.

Everyone would have long since forgotten the sect had the chroniclers not taken such pains to relate their misfortune.

< 30 >

KITO

Kito hardly knew what to think. For more than half a century, the Indian's finger had been poised above the red button on which was written: _____. He dared not breathe, nor even blink. What would be the consequences if he did dare? Kito slowly gathered his wits that were assembled in a half-circle around him. Half a century is a long time. Kito's task was arduous, and called for a healthy dose of insinuation. Maybe that button would have activated him, or someone else. But that was unlikely. Kito was alone. He lived in painful anticipation in the middle of the silent station, buried beneath two hundred meters of preislamic granite.

All is as quiet down here as it is on the surface. The mummy of the last president-for-life grimaces from behind the glass case where it has been displayed since the election of the last government. Kito the Indian does not move. With a great sense of duty, his finger is poised above the red button. He feels neither perplexed nor doubtful, only incongruous. Motivated by some inexplicable tremor. The irremediable has taken the form of a button. Two centimeters from his fingertip. From the end of the world. Here. Without recourse. Kito tries not to consider the consequences.

He has stopped fearing for his wife and children. He soars above all suspicion. Kito's voice seems changed, but it is pure. In one of his favorite visions, his children grow up in the shade of giant sequoias. The snow piles up on the roof of their home and wisps of smoke rise from the chimney. A wind off the mountain purifies everything, slowly, very slowly. By the sheer force of its obstinacy.

Kito waits in a state of suspicious impartiality. The jackdaw that returns to visit him each year can ask him a thousand times a day, "What? What? What for?" But he will wait. The jackdaw sometimes changes his perch. Never his words.

In his Indian soul, Kito knows that the earth will always find some kind of nourishment. What it might be, he dares not imagine. Resignation is his lot. He swims in the middle of the dark lake. The red button glimmers before him. Occupies the space. All the available space. And then everything stops.

< 32 >

NATASHA

Natasha was not alone. The crowd pressed against her and jostled her inconsiderately. She liked the contact, the hollow sounds her body made when it collided with other similar bodies. She felt part of that howling, exuding mass that passed through her in all directions. It was a heady feeling. She awakened and realized she had been dreaming. Her first thought was to go to her office, as she did each morning, and pick up the telephone to make sure there was no one on the other end of the line. She would say, "Hello! I'm listening." She repeated the code words three or four times, then waited a few seconds before putting down the handset.

She was old, almost as old and worn as the clothing on her back. She had been living here in the watchtower of the Desert of Ziph forever. She fell into confusion whenever she tried to calculate how long it had been. She didn't know. One hundred and fifteen years, maybe?

Her report indicated that she had arrived the same year as the election of the last government. At the time, Natasha Baldwin was young and ambitious. She had worked actively to help elect Lee Baldwin, the only candidate who ran in that post-historic election. The new president-for-life had rewarded her with a prestigious position in the public service. She was a border guard on the northeast periphery of the Desert of Ziph, several hundred kilometers north of the ancient city of Boston.

Lee Baldwin was a reprobate, and his calculations were bald-faced. His intention was to drive from the corridors of power the only person who could have challenged him. But that was not how Natasha saw things. Maybe the telephone line had been cut centuries ago, or maybe no one applied for permission to cross the border that separated Status from the Desert of Ziph since she had taken up her position. But she felt there must have been a reason for her job, and that it would be revealed to her, and her alone, one day. That was why she never lost heart. Every morning, before the sun struck the hilltops and began to soften all that it touched, she would inspect the six hundred and forty meters of road that seemed to point an accusing finger at the desert, and that ended abruptly at an immense, half-disintegrated concrete block. The road began and ended there. That is to say, nowhere. Then Natasha would make her way back to the watchtower at an almost martial pace that, she told herself, suited the seriousness of her functions.

Natasha set up her office, with the telephone as its centerpiece, in the horrible watchtower. She did not really live there. In the summer, the suffocating heat made it impossible to stay there more than thirty seconds, and in the winter, the cold and damp permeated the walls, making the tower even more inhospitable. A few weeks after her arrival, Natasha had built herself a mud hut in the shade of a rock a few steps from the road.

One day—it was a seventeenth of October, Natasha recalled—a bird flew over her shelter. She was able to observe it at length: a black bird with a killer's head, a crow perhaps. It silently circled overhead for several minutes before flying off with a caw of bewilderment. For some time, Natasha wondered if that arguably extraordinary occurrence was worth mentioning in her report. She could not make up her mind. From one point of view, the event seemed harmless. The bird had flown back toward the Desert of Ziph without having crossed the border. There was no reason to mention it in the report. But from another angle, the bird with the killer's head seemed clear proof that life was slowly returning to the Desert of Ziph, and Natasha did not know whether that was good news or bad. In any event, it was news. And there was not much of that. Natasha increased her vigilance level. She never took her eyes off the sky. Her mind was made up: if the bird (the same or another) came prowling hereabouts, if it crossed the border without the necessary authorization, she would not hesitate for an instant to denounce it in her report.

< 34 >

LEE

The roots were bitter, and increasingly hard to find. The ones that Lee dug up were spindly, or already half-devoured. To find his weekly ration, he had to travel ever further, and that meant venturing dangerously far from the bunker. It was a risk he had to take. There was no way around it.

The first time Lee Baldwin noticed something in the sky, he imagined the worst. That was always the first thing to do, in any circumstance. If you were to survive in this world, you needed to use that stratagem, and every day proved it.

Lee raised his head and saw them gliding at the edge of the vault of dark clouds that fitted like an iron lid on the kettle of the world. At first he thought they were vultures. Loathsome creatures that would gladly peck out his eyes if he took it into his head to sleep outside the bunker. He had seen vultures once, in a documentary film. But these vultures seemed unreal. They floated, motionless, at some distance from one another, and he could not say whether they were attracted by carrion or simply enjoying the upper air.

Lee watched them in the days that followed. The flock hovered above the same spot. Lee estimated that they were ten to fifteen kilometers south of his position. There were a dozen, maybe more. At that distance, he could not be sure.

He felt no urge to get closer. He watched, fascinated. The vultures never landed. "Maybe they sleep in the air," Lee speculated. He had seen that in the documentary film; he knew some migratory birds could do that. But vultures? "Vultures are not, I'm telling you, are not migratory birds."

Lee had never seen a kite in his life.

When Desmond's kite string broke, he wept hot tears. It was at the Tuttle country fair. The Ferris wheel glittered on the fairway among the multicolored tents and banners. His kite broke away from the flock and continued to ascend. The wind carried it north in uneven fashion. Desmond's father did his best to console him. He told the boy he would buy him another kite even bigger than the old one, more beautiful and faster. In his desperation, he offered him another ride on the merry-go-round, but Desmond would have none of it. He wanted his kite back, he bawled, he wanted his kite back, he wanted his kite back.

When the device crashed a few meters from the bunker, Lee jumped. He wasn't expecting anything like that. He approached the kite cautiously, and saw that one of its uprights had broken on impact, and that its cloth was ripped in places. A plastic tube containing a piece of paper was attached to the tail. He opened the tube and removed the message, unrolled it and ran his fingertip over it, line by line, from right to left, then from left to right, from top to bottom, then from bottom to top.

Lee Baldwin did not know it at the time, but he was holding the speech of the last president-for-life in his hands. It would take him a long time to decipher it, but he would succeed, and one day he would deliver it to an empty auditorium, in front of Natasha Baldwin, his sole elector.

< 36 >

LOTHAR

Grave robber. Such was the difficult, disproportional trade that made Lothar undertake his long, lonely journeys. He crossed desert regions so vast that millions of people could have lived there. Perhaps they had, but at some faraway, forgotten time. Lothar certainly had forgotten it. He never encountered anyone, nor did he come upon even the hint of a grave to rob. Not that he lacked the aptitude: Lothar's was remarkable. He could sniff out death from kilometers away. Lothar's flair had nothing to do with his failure. Simply put, Lothar had, over time, gotten lost. The landscape posted no map, indicated no direction; it provided no formal structure by which it could be deciphered. The landscape mocked Lothar; it recoiled from him. Wherever he went, whether he followed the sun or the moon, whether he walked barefoot or in sandals fashioned from coarse leather. The landscape continued to recoil, and Lothar was perplexed. At times, he would dig a random hole, just to satisfy himself. Often he would unearth things. Objects of no value, for the most part. But from time to time, by chance, he would come across a scrap of sheet metal. More rarely, a piece of polished glass or empty, rust-pierced tin cans. But tombs? No. Not a single one in more than a quarter-century. Hundreds of times, he almost gave up. He considered trading his profession for a less demanding one. He could have been a dentist, or a plumber. A veterinarian. He remembered a time when he'd dreamed of becoming a veterinarian. Just like everyone else. Like all the little Baldwins at the same age. But Lothar's fate was different. His calling was to be a grave robber, and that was what he became. His own tomb was never found. Which is why the report concerning Lothar remains incomplete to this day.

MAX

Max was his name. The Cyclopes pronounced it *Wax*, drawing out the final *x* forever, and they couldn't keep themselves from sticking out their hideous tongues, and wiggling about ecstatically while depositing bucketfuls of viscous sputum on the floor of his cell, which he later had to carefully swab up. Not only was it difficult work, but most of all Max feared the corrosive, hallucinogenic effects of Cyclops sputum.

It did not take much to get them excited.

As befits a Baldwin, Max found consolation wherever he turned. In his captivity. In his solitude. As a Baldwin, he was entitled to special treatment and certain advantages, and he would have felt guilty had he not enjoyed them to the fullest, considering the life expectancy of the members of his species. It was fifteen years at the most. But Max had already begun his twenty-sixth year, and he prided himself on his *performance*. (The report is quite insistent about this particular point, for no apparent reason.)

Max belonged to a certain Körch, the director of the Grand Körch Circus. He had purchased him during the seasonal auction at the Dharmaville growers' fair. Max owed everything to Körch, his beloved protector, whereas the latter had certainly made the most profitable transaction of his career by acquiring Max from a provincial wholesaler for a song.

Max had forgotten almost everything about his life on the battery farm where he was born. The only reminder of his childhood, and it was a furtive one at that, was the unctuous, vaguely familiar odor he would fleetingly pick up when the train that carried them from city to city, during the circus' endless tours, would pass close to a farm.

Thanks to the Grand Körch Circus, Max traveled extensively. On tour, they sailed the seas and landed in every port, from Ibavir to Andoska. At a rate of two performances a day, the circus gave no fewer than one thousand two hundred and thirty-six shows a year. For many years, Max's routine had been the Grand Körch Circus' main attraction. Delighted Cyclopes came from far and wide to watch him solve, upon request, the addition, subtraction and multiplication problems Körch had taught him: 24 + 24 = 2424; 56 – 6 = 5; 3 x 3 = 333. For Max, it was never more than a simple formality. He could press on and keep his public spellbound for hours on end. Arithmetic was an open book for him. He executed his routine with the greatest of ease, and the delighted audiences would never fail to show their satisfaction by noisily clicking their tongues. For the grand finale, he would draw several geometric figures on a blackboard at the front of the stage: a circle, a square, a triangle. He would cap his performance with a magnificent, perfectly symmetrical five-pointed star that he drew with one stroke, a moment of pure magic that marked the high point of the show. In the stands, excitement would reach a fever pitch. The spectators in the top rows would piss on those underneath them, who stomped wildly on the ground with their cloven clogs.

Max was blind. He had long since forgotten what our world looked like. He had vague memories of a light fixture, maybe two, with the impression of them capriciously changing positions in a turgid sky. The memory would fill him for a second or two, then he would forget.

Lately, his health had been declining. He felt a persistent pain in his left flank. Körch made up his mind to abandon him here, in the clinic, and the circus went on its way. "The show must go on," Körch had said.

Prior to our arrival at the clinic, Max had made overtures to the female patients only. Reckoning by his sense of touch, he discovered they were all young. Their breasts were firm and small, which would have convinced him of their puberty, but he also

< 39 >

found out that most of them had not yet had their eyes removed. That was eloquent testimony in itself.

Every night, the guard would lead a new, barely nubile female into Max's cell. It did not take him long to figure out what was expected of him, and he did his best to oblige. He was proud of the social prestige that being a stud conferred.

"I regret nothing," he made a point of saying. "Write that down in the report. Körch has been great, I don't know what I would have become without him. Mind you, that's just a figure of speech! I know exactly what I would have become without him! In any case, my days are numbered. I'm no fool. Last night they brought in another female, and I couldn't discharge my duties. That's the third time it's happened this week. The guard must have noticed. What the hell! My conscience is at rest. Körch promised, and I have his word: my corpse won't be dragged off to the cannery, as is the custom. No. Not Max! I deserve a place of honor in the Museum of Civilization! The museum's taxidermist has been informed. He'll transform me into the most striking tribute to Körch's genius, he, my beloved protector."

As a measure of his coquetry, they went to an Armilane jeweler to order the pair of glass eyes that would grace his sockets.

"Life has been good to me, truly good," Max insisted. "That should be the conclusion of your report."

And so it is.

< 40 >

Case Dismissed

This story may well speak of death. Either that, or something impossible that lies beyond. Maybe the chroniclers didn't have any choice in the matter. Funny thing, a story that begins at the end. But that's how it is.

Maybe death won't be mentioned in this story in so many words. There may be only distant references. We would really rather not see it come too close to our circle. But even if we try to avoid it, death is there. To be there, it really doesn't need much. It might appear in the way a young woman walks, or in a waiter's weary gesture as he pockets his tip or, thousands of kilometers distant, in the crushing of a wasp against the windshield of a 1979 Malibu.

Death really doesn't need much. No sooner is it placed at the beginning of the story (where it should never appear) than it takes up all the space, and the story itself vanishes into its shadow. That's one of its characteristics. Some are more irritating than others.

The most irritating thing about death is the way it just sits there, looking at you with utter indifference, or the way it has of saying that the chroniclers ought to shut up once and for all.

OTTO

Far below, on the plain, Otto waited, unmoving. His inert body was buried. Only his nose emerged from the reddish clay that covered him.

And Otto waited.

He had a gift for that.

To reach him, Sylvia had to cross Zone K 61. The worst of all. Past it lay the Desert of Ziph, and further beyond, the territories that were spoken of in low voices, and only in case of extreme necessity. Sylvia had to face constraints that were as perilous as they were unexpected. Once she even confronted a polar bear, but history does not relate if her victory over it was unequivocal, or due to the kind of subterfuge one might expect from her sex.

Still in all, she continued on her journey, convinced she was in the right, facing the dangers of frozen seas, scaling peaks thought to be insurmountable, making a mockery of the adversaries fortune had placed in her path. In her native village, legends about her were already being written. (It is said that each is more implausible than the last, but we cannot really assess them for they have all, alas, been forgotten.)

Only Otto's nose emerged from the ground. In fact, Otto had become nothing more than a nose. But a magnificent nose. An impregnable citadel. An organ so developed, so precise, it could detect a marriage of birds kilometers away, or a caravan of beggars long before the sands engulfed them.

Sylvia was still several hundred nautical miles away when, for the first time, he caught the young woman's unmistakable scent. Day by day he followed her approach, flowed into her arms, led her into the red muck where they would lose themselves in wild embrace. Otto knew he was doing himself harm, and might have taken even greater pleasure in imagining that things could actually unfold as he dreamed they would, even though death, for the moment and for some time now, seemed to have closed off every exit, one after another.

As for Sylvia, she trusted only her dreams. They left her no rest. One day, she spent hours contemplating one of them. It was a stunted dream: black pebbles emerged from a plain of reddish clay that extended as far as her eye could see. Looking closer, she saw that the stones were pulsing with the halting breath of life. Each possessed two orifices through which it could inhale. Looking closer still, she recognized Otto's nose. She could not have said how she recognized it, but her dream left her no doubt: it was Otto's nose, it was Otto's nose, it was Otto's.

Nose.

< 43 >

SHEIDA

In the times of which I speak, only one prostitute was registered in the entire northern hemisphere. Sheida Baldwin was her name, and she lived in the old warehouses in Zone D27. When she was young, she had been very beautiful, before the struggle for survival broke her. In those days, her skin did not conjure up old parchment. She had not turned grey, and she still smelled good: her sweat was tangy. It was invigorating, it inspired devilish concupiscence in you. Her particular fragrance was responsible for making her the toast of the town from Bangkok to Berlin. Her reputation was probably inflated, or at least that's what certain people claimed. Still, her clients were prepared to sacrifice everything to spend as little as a quarter-hour in her company. And the clients would come from everywhere. By the busload. They would get off at the entrance to the zone and, from there on, they were on their own. Endless processions of ragtag clients filed through the ruins in search of Sheida. The spectacle fascinated the zone's few inhabitants, and they could frequently be seen gathering at the crossroads to encourage the suitors, or give them false instructions about what direction to take. Many would simply quit after a time, but it was difficult to tell the serious, motivated clients from those who had given up trying to find the prostitute and were now hoping to flee the zone. They resembled one another so cruelly: the same concupiscent look in their eyes, the same foot-dragging gait, the same supplications and cries of dismay when the road opened onto a vacant lot strewn with useless memories, or an ocean black with deadly emanations, and they had to retrace their steps.

In the early years, Sheida had high hopes. But over time, she came to realize that none of the clients would ever find his way to her. Yet she used all her wiles to attract them, and point them in the right direction. She launched thousands of multicolored balloons into the blotchy sky. Other times, she tried flights of pigeons or smoke signals. Then there were the coded messages broadcast through the northern hemisphere. To no effect. Much later, she resigned herself. All the suitors had either died or fallen ill long ago, in the time of which I speak. One after the other, they passed away with a strange smile on their lips, as though they had found a certain contentment in the long pursuit of happiness. The unfulfillment that held them prisoner never kept them from singing her praises. Until the very end, Sheida Baldwin would remain the object of their adoration. They worshipped her until the final spasm that's still called death, for want of a better term.

And that's why, even though much time has passed since Zone D 27 was still indicated on the maps, the chroniclers enjoy recalling the memory of Sheida Baldwin, the prostitute of the northern hemisphere, and her valorous clients.

< 45 >

TOM

Lying in a puddle of sunlight, behind hangars 7 and 8, Tom blinked and stretched. Just that vague feeling of having been pulverized into a fine powder. No one would disturb him here, in this sanctuary. In front of him the hangars, left in shreds by the most recent storms, formed an impregnable rampart. On every side, imposing heaps of debris would slow the assaults of eventual invaders, while to the rear, the railway line held out the possibility of escape.

"Blessed are the vagrants," Tom thought, "for they … " But he never completed the phrase, either in thought or word. He did not bother. What was the use? Blessed are the vagrants: that was good enough.

The sun was hot, and the sheet metal on top of which Tom had lain for so long suddenly seemed uncomfortable. Perhaps he should move into the shade, over there, in the cabin with the broken windows that Tom liked to call the Observatory. There he might find the remains of a breeze. But for that, he would have to climb the one hundred and forty-seven rusted rungs of the iron ladder. Mentally he preferred to make his way around the Observatory and head toward the lake that lay on the other side of the railway line. It would not be so hot over there, but he would suffer the vicious and constant attack by the clouds of mosquitoes thirsting for fresh blood.

Tom Baldwin never wavered.

He sank more deeply into the puddle of sunlight that had already reached his knees, and he savored the passing seconds, minutes and hours as a cicada began thrumming furiously nearby. It never occurred to Tom that, with its delirious war cry, the cicada was claiming possession of the puddle of sun that he had squatted in without a second thought. It occurred to him even less that the camp commander had noted his disappearance several weeks before, and that now the search was on in Zone C 4.

No. Tom whiled away the hours placidly, and very little occurred to him. "Blessed are the vagrants!" Tom was one, and the other. He knew how to find the necessary peace and quiet. Since the beginning of the afternoon, Tom had been meticulously picking his nose and placing the finest specimens on the piece of sheet metal, where he watched them bake.

"I have rights," he would say from time to time, "inalienable rights."

Who would dare contradict him?

< 47 >

OGATA

For a prison guard, Ogata was short-legged. He would scoot down the prison corridors, inexplicably propelled by his puny limbs. He never missed a turn, and never let himself be distracted. He was an affable prison guard for whom it was a point of honor to provide his customers with courteous, polite and attentive service.

For all that, he was unhappy! The prison had long since been deserted. All that Ogata guarded now were the fissured, moldering walls, overgrown with vegetation that seemed to negate them. To negate even their memory.

The prison had been uninhabited since the year the last government was elected. Ogata could remember that year, as he could remember his last prisoner, who had been pardoned by Lee Baldwin the day he took office. Though some days Ogata would forget the name of his singular beneficiary, he could easily and pleasurably recall the feeling he had as he watched him come to life in his cell. Now that had been a prisoner, big as life. The kind of prisoner a prison guard can only dream about. A rare bird. A brute, a bundle of justifiable rage.

The prisoner—his name came back to him now, it was Malcolm—could not remember what he'd been accused of. His file did not spell out the charges, nor whether there had been one or many. Perhaps there had been none at all. The file contained no mention of disciplinary problems, even during his long terms in Lisbon, and later, on the island of Vanuatu. Not the slightest lapse was noted. Only an assumed name, the date of his entry and that of his release. Between the two dates, three or four tiny, vulgar sketches, doodling that could no doubt be attributed to an underemployed civil servant.

The report contained nothing else.

Had Malcolm committed some crime, perhaps his victim had expunged both the crime and its consequences from his memory, as well as its author. That was a distinct possibility. Malcolm had been imprisoned for so long that it was impossible to trace the river of his life to its source. The source of that river, so wide that those who lived on its shores called it the sea—for they could catch sight of the opposite shore only in very clear weather, and even then, only through a shimmering curtain of mist and whalesong—may have been no more than a rivulet of dirty water flowing between two mossy rocks into a hollow where it lay stagnant for centuries before filtering down, always further down, to the sea.

So it was that Ogata, instead of guarding his prisoner, preserved his memory. The memory of prisoner Malcolm working hard to do nothing at all, living in perfect freedom in the heart of slumber harder than diamonds—that memory moved him deeply. For Ogata it was an act of faith, a way, equivocal perhaps, of resisting the slow progress of the vines and tendrils of ivy that laid siege to the ruins of the prison.

Ogata felt much better the day he came upon the idea of duplicating himself, so he could be both the prisoner and his indefatigable guard. He moved into the cell that had been vacant since the liberation of Malcolm Baldwin. He crossed his ridiculous limbs, squatted cross-legged and contemplated the decaying wall in front of him.

Beyond the prison walls, the world was proving to be hostile. There could be no doubt about it. Ogata was sure that, one day, Malcolm would grow weary of his futile freedom and want to return to his cell, no matter the cost. It was inevitable.

For the longest time, Ogata awaited the return of prisoner Malcolm. All sorts of complicating constraints crowded into

< 49 >

Ogata's head. What if Malcolm lost his way? What if he wandered into the marshes of eastern Ziph? Or worse, what if he had forgotten his attentive, devoted guard, what if he had struck from his memory the very recollection of his term in prison? It was a risk to be taken. It was terrible to think about, but all possibilities had to be considered: perhaps Malcolm Baldwin had never existed.

< 50 >

MAGALI

When the chroniclers remember her name—which happens frequently enough—they prefer to call her the Dreamer, but her birth name is Magali. Magali has more than a few names, of course. Each of them inextricably linked to a facet of her personality. But the chroniclers have their reasons for focusing their attention on this one. Some say it's due to the exact angle of the declination of the moon. The hour at which its light is most fertile.

Magali: another way of saying it.

In this place, infinitely hidden from the prying glances of strangers, Magali is also a young girl who collects chrysalises, who cares lovingly for the little larvae, keeping them warm until the time comes for their metamorphosis. This is her way of saying that colonization must begin again. Her personal response.

In winter, Magali has difficulty imagining the sun. But if it were there, she wouldn't believe she could have forgotten it. Yet this is exactly what happens most of the time with the sun, and with plenty of other phenomena: surrogate mothers and sperm donors. In her dreams, the Dreamer has entire herds of brothers and sisters that she broods ferociously in the attics of abandoned buildings.

The day the inspector authorized by Indian Affairs discovered Magali, he dared not awaken her. The chrysalises were rapidly counted and the sarcophagi closed again.

Another way of saying it.

GRETCHEN

According to the report, Gretchen appeared at the watchmaker's shop on the thirty-ninth of November of that year. "I've come for my heart" were her first hopeful words, but the watchmaker was nobody's fool. He insisted on Gretchen telling her story from the beginning.

The personal legend of Gretchen Baldwin turned out to be disgustingly banal. She grew up in Baltimore during the last ice age, and married a second-class Baldwin. The couple was sterile. Gretchen had to resign herself and relinquish her embryos to the bank, and the interest did not allow her to make a decent living. The husband became an erotomaniac and ended up suffocating in a plastic bag. Gretchen found him dangling sadly at the end of a leash. Add to this family portrait an incestuous, alcoholic father, a child-murdering mother plus the usual parade of hereditary malevolence and deficiencies.

Gretchen never had a chance.

But that wasn't what dislocated her heart. Something else was to blame. She didn't know what.

Today, warm and toasty in the old cardboard boxes that she built into a shelter, Gretchen reminisces. As she does, she never unclenches her teeth. She stares straight ahead, and will not see anything at all. Or say anything at all. She will almost forget who she is. She'll wish that everything would just stop.

The watchmaker would sincerely like to help her. Contradict her on certain points of detail, such as the date of their appointment or the relevance of an infanticidal mother. Point out to her that such things are impossible. But Gretchen has stopped moving.

It would be wrong to say she's dead.

LORI

Dear Lori,

I am writing you from the front window of my room, the one that overlooks the alley behind the fish store. I am writing you to ask, "What is critical mass?"

> *Critical mass*: a mass of sufficient size to sustain
> or to be capable of sustaining a chain reaction.

What does that mean, Lori?

Maybe you don't see the big hole it makes in me. Right here. Maybe you don't want to see it. *Sustaining a chain reaction.* It says what it means, right?

You're right: we needed more light at our last meeting. It was cold, too. Not exactly snow in July, but something like that. Something out of place. You were wearing the grey wool coat that suits you so well, the one that makes you look as if you were floating far above us all, above the whole town.

You know you don't have to shrug your shoulders that way.

You don't have to tell the truth.

Or even know it.

Or always know what to do or think.

You've got the right to be wrong.

No common denominator.

No answer.

Maybe no survival.

It's the same story every time, Lori.

SERGEI

The last time he'd met him, he called himself Tonino. Tonino Baldwin. But once they reversed roles, Tonino didn't know his real name was Sergei. That didn't keep him from hesitating a final moment. From the top of the dam, he watched the sun drop into the sea like a lead casting. This was a unique opportunity for existence, he told himself, then he let himself be swept away by the current.

Sergei's nearest neighbor lived two or three thousand posts from his place. A certain Tonino. So claimed the prospectus. Sergei had never seriously considered making the trip. Until that day when, many years later, the winds became favorable. Then he leaned a final time against the guardrail high above the dam and looked out over the emptiness that stretched as far as the eye could see: not a single drop of water. The monstrous device slumbered beneath the concrete rubble. The croak of a vulture grated against the sky. There was no reason for concern. On his own, Tonino would not have known how to switch on the turbines. He did not know, and so the idea of doing it never crossed his mind.

He took to the air. He needed only three steps, then he flung himself headfirst into the void. On the way down, hot breath burned his eyes.

One after another, the Baldwins tore themselves free from the earth. No one tried to hold them back.

Once airborne, Sergei gave no thought to his direction. (Once you begin, you must never consider stopping; the craft rockets forward at stupendous speed.) Sooner or later, he told himself, he would detect some form of life. He told himself it was yet another unique opportunity for existence. And he was perfectly right. It was indeed one.

Sergei wasn't sure he had replaced the cover of his subconscious. Reality seemed to carry less and less weight. Neither the mountains nor the sky had the required consistency. That slight flaw immediately disqualified everything.

His flight lasted no more than six or seven minutes. All eternity.

Since then, by day and by night, in all seasons, perched on the edge of his hole, Sergei has been awaiting the sun. At night, he shivers and curls up at the bottom of the hole. But during the day, he reckons the real position of the sun behind the thick ashen clouds that stream above his head. From time to time, a fugitive ray pierces the cloudy vault, and Sergei bathes in its light.

The sun is so strong that Sergei has to close his eyes, the better to look at it. Only the sun—and these are its last moments—only the sun could know nothing about justice.

He had no idea which way to go. The prospectus contained no clues. He knew nothing, but he headed there all the same. Maybe that was the crux of his tragedy.

The report does not specify how long Sergei's journey lasted, nor even if his meeting with Tonino ever took place. It does not mention any of the subterfuges Sergei was forced to use to reach his goal, nor even if he had one. Quite simply, the chroniclers refuse to say anything more about Sergei Baldwin.

< 55 >

CHRISTOPHE-BENJAMIN

Sometimes I still wonder if I really chose Christophe-Benjamin, or if he chose me. It was the year of all disappointments, long after the great tsunami and the downpours that followed. No one knew exactly when. There were almost no valid reasons for keeping track.

It's true. No one should have survived all that. But what were we supposed to do? People hang on. We can't really criticize them. They want to keep walking in the sun, even if it's not there any more, even if it's been forgotten. They keep doing it. It's perfectly legitimate.

I recovered Christophe-Benjamin across from Building A that day, just before nightfall. When I think about it—and it's highly unlikely for me to do that—I say to myself that I nearly missed seeing him at all. Christophe-Benjamin came drifting by on a makeshift raft hastily assembled during the last deluge.

At first I thought he was dead. I tried to grab hold of the leather bag he had over his shoulder. He must have awakened when I grazed him with the long pole I used to try to snare the bag, since he turned and threw me the dark stare of scorn and ingratitude I had become so familiar with over the years. As I worked to slip the leather sack from the old man's shoulder, I realized he was not quite dead. And that he who would snatch his bag had not yet entirely been born.

The first thing we had to do, Christophe-Benjamin and I, was stare into the whites of one another's eyes. We couldn't avoid it. Christophe-Benjamin relaxed when he understood I had nothing against his bag. He grabbed onto the pole and I pulled him onto my raft. By the time we'd finished our acrobatics, we were both soaked to the skin.

Christophe-Benjamin was in such a derelict state I was sure he wouldn't survive the winter. He grunted something: a word of encouragement or a revolutionary song? Hard to tell.

I brought him home. I did it without thinking twice, the way I would have with any piece of debris worthy of my interest or desire.

Building A was big enough for two. As well, we had full use of Building B, with its three floors that were still above water (a lot less spacious than A, seven floors of which were completely empty).

In Building A, before Christophe-Benjamin arrived, there was no one but me. Me and the Smoke, that is. But most of the time the Smoke never moved, hidden in a crack in the wall facing the main entrance. I'd repaired the trap door—it was nearly invisible—and even provided a tiny peep-hole so the Smoke could watch my comings and goings.

The Smoke didn't react when I showed up with Christophe-Benjamin. That surprised me, and I don't surprise easily. I had set him in front of the main entrance to Building A, hoping he'd function as an alarm system, or at least as a doorbell—in case of invasion—and I'd been looking for the chance to see how good he'd be. Maybe he didn't think the test was worthwhile, since I was with Christophe-Benjamin. But maybe the Smoke hadn't understood at the time, any more than I had, that Christophe-Benjamin was dangerous.

It didn't take long for me to have second thoughts about saving Christophe-Benjamin from the icy waters. I dropped him on the second floor, and he started to dry off. Then he emptied the contents of his bag: a bamboo flute, a pair of scissors, a ball of twine, a small package of feathers and a large folder containing a sheaf of yellowed sheets of paper. All of it perfectly dry, rolled up in plastic bags.

But nothing to eat.

Through the half-open door, I watched him set up his survival mechanism. He spread the sheets of paper on the floor and placed them in circles. They formed groups, arabesques, still-

< 57 >

smoldering volcanoes. When I looked more closely, I could see the microscopic signs that covered the pages: they seemed to recreate undecipherable labyrinths bursting with ink. Christophe-Benjamin methodically placed the sheets across the full width of the room. The operation took several hours. One by one, he laid them in different spots, as if trying to reconstitute their original order. But either he had forgotten that order, the one he had been working to recover all these years, or there had never been one in the first place. Christophe-Benjamin hesitated.

I waited till the next day to go into the room. Christophe-Benjamin was sleeping peacefully, curled up in a ball in the least filthy part of the floor. He used his bag as a pillow, and some tattered pages as a blanket.

I could have decided to end it right there. Put a stop to it all. Period. But I preferred to let events take their course in their chosen order. It's one of my personality defects I have to live with.

I've been saving Christophe-Benjamin at the same time for too many years now. He clings to the pole I stretch out to him, and I drag his emaciated body from the water. He groans feebly. According to the rules of simple decency, I should rough him up a little. Anyone else would do it. Anyone. But I just pull him onto my raft and bring him back to my place. I offer him a second life that he may not even want, I drag him up from the nothingness into which he was sinking, joyless, but of his own volition. That, you see, is the strange thing about Christophe-Benjamin: he actually exhibits a will of his own.

But not now. Not while he lies sleeping at my feet.

I examine the sheets of paper. They're covered with strange signs. I say strange because they seem both obscure yet familiar. I've already seen signs like these. I've seen them often enough to know I'm dealing with a writer. And that's what's been worrying me from the start.

Before Christophe-Benjamin showed up, the choppers rarely came this far. But on the first nights, there were whole swarms of them, playing their spotlights along the perimeter. The deafening

< 58 >

din of the turbines and the muffled hammering of the rotors as they whipped through the air did not even awaken Christophe-Benjamin. In the morning, I often heard him moaning, complaining about having been stung by hordes of mosquitoes or awakened suddenly by a rat-bite, but he never heard the choppers. Some nights, they ventured right up to his window, and their spotlights swept the floor where Christophe-Benjamin slept. Maybe the scribbling on the paper was so insignificant that they couldn't make it out, or maybe they too felt the danger that Christophe-Benjamin represented. In any case, the choppers moved off after a while.

Like everyone else, I knew that scribblers were outlawed. They had been for so long that you could hardly believe some still survived. I soon began believing that Christophe-Benjamin was the last. The very last of the scribblers. And that I would lose the quiet existence that had been mine up until then.

I never dared ask him to let me blow a few notes on his little bamboo flute. I knew that only trouble could come from a writer's flute—or propositions for trouble, if nothing else. But I wanted to understand what he was doing on the raft that morning, and I communicated that to him in sign language.

"This dark passageway, through which someone is breathlessly running," I suggested off the top of my head, "perhaps it is I." (To get things going, I could have done better, but Christophe-Benjamin seemed to appreciate my frankness.)

Once, of course, I asked him about the eternal ice, and the possibility of actually visiting the ice cap, but his face hardened. He was much more loquacious when I mentioned the persistent rumors about the eventual colonization of the Andean archipelago. That information seemed to pique his interest. He wanted to know more. Which is why I questioned him as often as I could about the subject. Every time I had the opportunity, to be exact.

Until then, I spent the better part of my time scanning the horizon, that indistinct, wavering line where the sky turned up and wrinkled, and where the waters boiled, no doubt. From now

< 59 >

on, I told myself, I'd better keep one eye on the horizon and the other on Christophe-Benjamin.

Moved by my impartial gaze, I didn't expect him to open up and start inscribing all manner of strange signs on the walls of Building A, but that's exactly what happened in the seventeenth month of that year. When I awoke that morning, the signs were already visible on three floors. Christophe-Benjamin had written them on the walls and the ceilings, and he was about to attack the floors and the elevator shaft.

I got there too late. On their next fly-over, the choppers would be sure to see them. Maybe the satellite had already detected and interpreted them. Christophe-Benjamin was like that. He liked to take risks. I guess it was a fundamental trait of any writer worthy of the name. The only problem with Christophe-Benjamin is that he put the lives of those near and dear to him at risk without even realizing it.

I remember an event that took place around the same time. The Smoke threw himself off his perch, fracturing his collarbone and suffering multiple contusions. I was forced to put the unfortunate creature's suffering to an end, and recover his *critical mass*; the tomatoes and beans I grew on the roof of Building B had never been tastier than that year. Even Christophe-Benjamin noticed the difference. He commented on the affair with a grunt that recalled the Smoke's devotion and sense of duty. Afterward, we never brought up the matter of the Smoke again. Those were hard times, and we knew how to appreciate them.

Christophe-Benjamin put out to sea a few days after the harvest. I helped him build his raft, then launch it. I think he just wanted to spare me any more trouble.

The choppers return now and then to scout the perimeter. They do it without much conviction. They examine the signs left by Christophe-Benjamin, as if they thought they might have a chance of understanding their meaning. Generally, after a while they leave, spiteful at having deciphered nothing, but happy they don't have to get involved.

< 60 >

LANDRIO

Landrio was a forest ranger. The forests had vanished long ago, of course. But Landrio was a forest ranger all the same. That was his official title, his occupation, his vocation, his trademark; it was written, engraved upon him at heights no one would have expected. Landrio spent most of his time patroling what had once been Forestry Exploitation Sector Q12, some of the roughest terrain in the northern zone. After all these years, he still hoped to discover some life form within the perimeter he had been assigned the year the last government was elected. But he was constantly hungry, and resist though he might, hunger would always overcome him. The increasingly rare lichen he scratched from the rocks could only half-satisfy his appetite. He remembered certain times when he would have gladly swallowed rocks to calm his hunger; he had forgotten that he'd already done just that.

Quite inexplicably, the event occurred on the seventeenth of Octemter of that year. For Landrio, in its multiple consequences, it had all the impact of an intimate cataclysm of exponential magnitude. Overnight, the forest sprang up. Landrio had not seen it coming. It swept in from the west like a devastating cavalry charge, and took root exactly where it had been. Right there.

The following day, at dawn, everything disappeared again.

Landrio wanted to believe it was all a dream, but knew that wasn't the case. All was crystal clear in his mind: he had felt the fine drops of night-time dew dripping from the young trees on his fingertips; he had been rocked by the wind sighing in the branches; he had breathed in the powerful odor of moist, overexcited soil.

The smell of life—you can tell it a mile away.

Now and again, since that day, Landrio will stretch out his arms. Were someone to come upon him in that position, he would swear that with one hand he was touching the sun and with the other, the moon. Nonetheless, it will be recorded that when all things came to an end, Landrio was found in that very position.

< 62 >

LENA

The pigeon on the fifth floor window ledge stared long and hard at Lena with its yellow eye, unwilling to take to the air. Maybe because of the gusts of wind, so strong today. That's it. Maybe he's afraid of the wind, Lena thought.

She looked up at the low-hanging sky, the boarded-up houses, the collapsed walls that were barely recognizable, the shreds of cloth fluttering in the wind, the smoke rising here and there, the hulks of vehicles, a swing squeaking threateningly, mud-spattered militiamen marching by in boots too big for them, a widening pool of blood, heaps of debris, hard to say what it is, shattered windows, the stink of burning rubber, electrical wires writhing in the street, a picture of fear and surprise.

When the frightened pigeon finally flew off, Lena averted her eyes.

It seemed to her like the thing to do.

TASHA

Don't you look nice with that big tousled head of yours! Cute, even, you little bundle of fur and purr! Just where did you pop up from? My name is Tasha. I'm going to be nine in seventeen minutes, and I've been burning my eyes this morning, staring at the sun. I love surprises, but I don't like to wait and burn my eyes staring at the sun. I was all by myself until you showed up on my park bench, you know. Just a minute ago, everything was quiet here, but now there are all kinds of people sitting on the grass, burning their eyes staring at the sun. I don't know where they came from. An old satyr asked me if I was lost. Do I look like I'm lost? He got a little too close, the old geezer, and he stunk like a tavern floor. So I looked him straight in the eye, like Mom taught me to. That caught him off guard, all right, and he said, "Excuse me, missy," then he turned on his heels and went off tongue-tied. Now he's sitting on a bench at the other end of the park, and he keeps looking over his shoulder to see if I'm still here.

I'm still here.

Burning my eyes staring at the sun.

The satyr was scared, I think, and it really rattled him not to know what he was scared of. A little girl who's going to be nine years old in sixteen minutes. You're not scared of anything, fuzzy-wuzzy, and it looks like you've just come back from a night on the town! It's not so smart to hang around here! You could get picked up, or worse, you could get knocked off by the Securitate guys. They take their jobs seriously. It's different for me. I'm just doing what Mom said to. She told me to wait here while she ran her errand.

Mom is black, and Pop says she's a real panther. He says that because she's black. But I think the panther part is in her eyes.

I'm chocolate, not black! Pop says I'm his favorite panther. Funny he should say that, 'cause I know it's Mom, not me, I know that much. But he tells such nice lies, and he tickles me so much that I forget to breathe, and then I turn chocolate pink!

The three of us together, we make a winning team. Even if Pop isn't black. Don't hold it against him, Mom says, it's not his fault. Nobody's perfect. That's what Mom says!

What a fool!

Before she went to meet Pop, she told me to keep an eye on the main entrance. See it, fuzzy-wuzzy? It's the one in the middle, under the big clock. She'll be coming through that door from the Presidential Palace, on Pop's arm. Kids aren't allowed in the Palace, even kids who are going to be nine years old in twelve minutes, especially not today when the president-for-life is receiving his acolytes for lunch. And you're nothing but a ball of flab and grease, so they wouldn't let you in either, no way!

Look! I can't believe it! Another one! That makes twelve limousines since I got here. They all stop under the clock above the main entrance, and a whole gang of Lilliputians comes piling out like they were going to be late for a very important date. Men in black open the limo doors, then other men in black get out and go up the stairs. I noticed something strange: the calmer the men in black who get out of the black limos look, the more nervous the men in black who open the doors seem to be. They scurry after them, carrying their black suitcases. Every now and then they stop, look around, left and right—you can't tell what they're looking for—then they start scurrying around like ants again. Black ants. Sometimes they put a hand to their ear as if they were listening to the sounds of the city. Their lips move like crazy and they lean over the banister, or look off into the distance, shading their eyes with their hands like Apaches. Pop says they're hired gorillas. He's always exaggerating. Even if they act strange, they look real enough. I can imagine that under their black suits they're wearing a thick coat of hair, black hair, maybe they're ashamed of being gorillas and that's why they're wearing masks. Maybe that's why they keep putting their hands to their ears:

< 65 >

they're adjusting their masks that keep wanting to slip off. That's what I think.

We're not from around here. You aren't either, my little fuzzy-wuzzy, as far as I can tell. Otherwise you wouldn't be curled up on my park bench. We're terrorized, Mom says, and I believe her. That's because we've got plenty of cash money in our family unit. The hideout in the neighborhood, a shack up near Lake Bouchette. You should come up there one of these days. You'd like it, it's our little bit of paradise. We've got trout this long, and creepy-crawlies scooting in and out of their holes. I just know you'd love it. It's nice and quiet. Not like here. No satyrs. No cops.

Look, fuzzy-wuzzy, there's one (a cop, I mean) talking to that satyr from before. I'd like to know what they're talking about. If I was a cop, I'd tell him to move on. Or lock him up, fast!

I'll never be a cop. I'm going to be nine years old in nine minutes, and that's for keeps. Mom says that cops on three continents are after us. That's why we're holding the other two back, the ones Pop calls "virgin lands," meaning they haven't been *raped* yet. Of course, those continents (Autarky and Aphasia, if I'm not mistaken) aren't really virgin. They've got car bombs there, too, oppressed people and any number of dirty old men, like everywhere else. But for us, they're virgin, get it? Because we haven't set foot there yet. Pop says we've got to fight turbo-liberalism any way we can. Turbo-liberalism is where it's at these days. It's the best way to exploit people so they'll never even notice, that's what Pop told me. It's a little complicated, a way of making them poorer while promising them they'll get richer. Get it? Quite a trick, right? What do you say, fuzzy-wuzzy? Anyway, it's working. One thing's for sure, people don't much like us, me and my family.

They're all ingrates, the whole lot of them. We're going to all this trouble for them, plus we don't have any fixed address, like they say.

Pop promised me fireworks for my birthday. He said they'd be the finest anybody's ever seen north of the 45th parallel, since the

< 66 >

last government got elected. Pop knows all about fireworks. He at least got that much out of the four years he spent in the special forces. He reached the top of his trade, and now he's one of the world's biggest fireworks experts.

At the beginning of his career, Pop had some important customers, high-class people, but one day he got fed up with their bad manners. High-class people are rude. You didn't know that? Nowadays, Pop works for himself (that means he's an independent contractor), and we have lots more fun than before. Plenty of travel, too. Every hick town we show up in, we set off tons of fireworks.

I used to go to school, but that was a long time ago. I went for a whole morning. Don't ask me how the other kids do it, they trot off in the morning, they trot back in the afternoon. Pop says they have to keep going because they didn't get it the first time. But you, you fuzzy little devil, I bet you never even got near a school! Can you imagine, they only teach you one of the 34 alphabets used in Andoska! Mom teaches me herself when she has the time. And let me tell you, we really have fun. Holy inquisitions, revolutions, wars of independence, universal declarations: you name it, we've done them!

Watch out, my furry friend! The cop's headed this way. Followed by the stinky old satyr, and they're sure not coming to wish me happy birthday. He's six minutes too soon for that. The cop looked bigger from further away. More like a baby cop. He doesn't even have a mustache—not very scary. Hey, now's no time to take off. Stick with me. We'll show 'em!

See, I'm looking the cop straight in the eye, just like Mom taught me to, but it's not working like it did with the satyr. You do what you can, right? "So," I say to him, "you're working for the turbo-liberals, is that it? Globalization, that's all you care about, huh? I bet you don't even know what it means! You don't even have a mustache. Isn't that what makes a cop a cop?"

That sure took the wind out of his sails. Just look at the expression on his face, his mouth sagging open from the crap I just made him swallow. The satyr's egging him on, elbowing him

< 67 >

in the ribs, but the baby cop doesn't care for the familiarity. Appearance is everything for him, no doubt about it, and he wants to keep his dignity in spite of the gaping hole I've just blasted in his respectability. But he's the proud type. To counter-attack, he tries to stare me down. Isn't that just like a cop, playing the big shot? "So, doll," he says, stroking me with the tip of his nightstick, "you're all alone? Lost, maybe? Is that your tomcat? What are you hiding in that box?" That's more than enough questions for one day, don't you think so? Wait, where are you going? So that's it! That's all it takes to send you packing, my ferocious feline? And I thought nothing scared you!

At that very moment, I knew I would be nine years old for the last time in my life. I opened the shoebox that had been sitting on my knees since early in the morning. The cop leaned over, and when he saw what was in the box, he took a step back. The satyr figured out what was about to happen, and just like that, he made himself scarce. All I had to do was press the button to get my totally awesome birthday fireworks display, just like Pop promised. I told you, my ninth birthday would be one to remember!

Okay, so maybe Mom and Pop got carried away a little more than usual, maybe even a lot more than they planned. I don't know. I never saw them again after that.

Still, the three of us really kicked the shit out of turbo-liberalism! Right?

< 68 >

FRANCINE

The postman was exhausted, and he looked dehydrated. Francine gave him a handful of grass to chew on, and let him rest on her bed in the shade of the bunker. She waited a little more for the postman to recover the use of his consciousness. In the meantime he grazed away and paid no attention to Francine's life and times.

She wondered how old he could be. About sixty, she figured. Travel keeps you young, Francine said to herself. Under his cap the postman was completely bald, though a long beard circled his neck like a grey scarf. He was a real postman, straight out of the catalogue, only dirtier. A used postman, you could say. The kind of out-of-date model you'd forget in some darker part of the basement.

Francine nipped into the bunker and popped right out again, catalogue in hand, trying to locate the corresponding image. The resemblance was remarkable. Only one detail bothered her: the letter bag. The postman in the catalogue proudly displayed his, while her postman had none. Maybe he'd lost it along the way. Maybe someone had stolen it. Maybe, in the end, exhausted, at the end of his rope, he'd left it near some rock, or thrown it down a dry well.

Francine couldn't wait to ask the postman a few questions. But he was sated from chewing on grass, and now he was lost in a deep sleep. She would have to wait until next spring before she could learn anything. At night, she watched over her postman. She tried to drag him inside the bunker, but he was much too heavy, and she had to give up. She built a lean-to quite like her own, with a fan that could be operated by a gentle pull of her big toe, thanks to an ingenious system of ropes and pulleys. During the day, she moistened the postman's lips on the hour to make sure he didn't become a nesting ground for colonies of snakes and scorpions, and she moved him every so often to create the illusion of an organic mass.

All the while, Francine hoped that her postman would soon be in no position to harm her, but she was fooling herself.

One day in April of that year, he shook himself from his procrastination and handed Francine an envelope. She had no idea where it could have come from, since she'd searched the postman from head to toe more than once. It was a brown, stained envelope with no return address, and it smelled moldy. It was addressed to a certain Itsuko Baldwin, in Buenos Aires. Francine looked around, and figured this place could very well have been called Buenos Aires at some point in the past. This place, or some other place. She understood immediately that there was no cause for fear, nor need to blush at the sound of her name. She unsealed the envelope, unfolded the letter and began to decode the signs, one at a time.

It was a request that Itsuko Baldwin contribute generously to a fund-raising campaign for an association that helped women who were victims of violence. But that was not what Francine understood.

Though a woman (or perhaps several) may have written these signs, they betrayed no hint of violence. They were, in fact, almost elegant.

One by one, Francine took the signs and arranged them in a different order. That maneuver changed the perspective dramatically. Now, in the letter, one of the women screamed in a heartbreaking voice, another pleaded to be left in peace, a third begged for alms on a deserted street corner, and the fear was perfectly visible, an abject fear in the depths of her fleeting gaze.

Francine abandoned her postman and took to the road the very next day.

< 70 >

THE BALDWIN KIDS

Everybody knows how ferocious the Baldwin kids are. They have pointed, sharp-edged teeth embedded in powerful jaws. Generally speaking, their dental apparatus seems more designed for tearing, biting and shredding than for chewing food. They're tenacious, too, the Baldwin kids. People say that all five of them gang up to down a wild boar, and cling to his trunk-like neck and bite through his jugular as the beast is emptied of its blood, of which not a drop is lost.

Those who have witnessed the event at least once can tell you that it creates a sense of disgust difficult to overcome, and that it is better to keep your distance until the end of the bloodletting. Once they have committed the act, the kids go back to their games, and to anyone watching them with naïve eyes, they become children again, touching in their innocence and in the grace of their movements.

But let a wild boar wander onto their playground, and their true nature comes to the fore.

HERMINA

Even today, people wonder how Hermina managed to last as long as she did. Did anyone ever think of asking her? They never put it into words. And this is what Hermina would not have told them: that it was their fault if, over time, she developed an affinity with the mineral realm, and now her crystalization was imminent, no doubt about it. Begun in the morning of the world, the process concluded as its night fell.

For Hermina, ultimate liquefaction in a fiery furnace of magma represented one possible nirvana. At first, she was confused. She realized, in a certain way, that she was the hermetically sealed channel for a multitude of voices that rose up within her, but that never found a way out, the one and only term, the final borborygmus that would, in masterful and definitive fashion, express all the others.

Her flowing, silver hair is wind-blown no more. She clings to the damp cliff face, a stubborn vine with innumerable ramifications, an antenna turned toward the most elementary caution, slowly extending her silence around her, catching the shreds of speech circulating in all directions and restoring them in some deteriorated, vulgar form.

Her speech, her own true speech, if she could ever make herself heard, would be salacious. Which is why she's happy to mouth the standard, time-tested formulas.

At noon, the sun will flare up with infantile, gratuitous cruelty. For Hermina, liquefaction will then become possible, though unlikely. For the voices grow hard within her, they turn to stone in the rarefied air that circulates in her lungs, but with ever-increasing difficulty. Soon she won't be equal to the constant effort of blocking out the buzz and hiss of the last government's speeches, of shutting them off once and for all, travestying them, giving them meaning they never had, but that might fortuitously, almost inadvertently, injure the enemy, like a stray bullet.

No one knows why, but the chroniclers still linger on Hermina's petrified lips. How naturally they assume that position, as if they had been trained for that very purpose, as if they were sitting by the mouth of a long-lifeless volcano.

The modesty of their bearing provokes envy among the anemones.

That's one more aporia.

< 73 >

SARA

The rain had been falling for forty years. No more than that.

Some of the world's loftiest peaks still stood above the surface. The Dayak, that famous homeopathic moon with its ghostly airs, had been reduced to a floating island. There was little chance of encountering it on the Great Sea that covered the globe. That embraced it. Strange things were happening in its depths, no one could hear the echo, but the imperceptible tremors had become more frequent. One day, something would have to emerge from the waters. Judging from the extent of things, it was clear that forces were at work in the unimaginable deep, but no one dared venture a guess as to what it might be, or what it might mean.

Survivors were few. Most wore masks. Some listened intently, and heard only the incessant slap of the Great Sea as it crashed against the shore. Many went mad. Even the wind stopped blowing over that watery world. If a bird happened to reach our island, it would stay for good.

The birds had a sizeable advantage over us: when water finally submerged the island, they could fly off to another place to reproduce. It was an equitable situation for them, but not for us. No one complained, but everyone placed their hopes in the improbable appearance of the Dayak, the floating island that would have let us continue our journey.

There was a time when Sara could still find eggs on the cliffside, but the birds had long departed, and the cliff itself had vanished. The water was now reaching for her thighs. At any moment, a more daring wave would lap at her sex.

The horizon had not yet slipped away. Sara stood between sky and sea. She wondered which of the two would crush her when the final attack came.

She hoped it would be the sky.

< 75 >

MIGWASH

Migwash would leave for work when the siren split the night. He was crew chief at the Ruthville landfill site. His workmates called him Mig but his girlfriend, if he'd had one, would have called him Migwasha.

"One day," Migwash said to himself, "I'll move far away from here, far from the mines, the foundries, the toxic waste disposal sites and the nuclear plants. I'll have a life of my own." Nothing would hold him back, his mind was made up. He would be a free man with a life of his own, maybe even a girlfriend. Maybe the thin girl who worked at the roadhouse. "Her, or another prettier one."

Migwash spotted the ant around noon on the seventeenth of September of that year. It was a red ant, a common ant, one of the kind that helped found the New World millions of years before, if not earlier, and that had every right to be where it was.

He squatted on the hard-packed earth floor of his shack to observe it. Was it disoriented, or had it set out in search of something that Migwash couldn't imagine? Maybe the ant was asking itself the same question, but there was no way of knowing. The image of the thing it sought was projected on its miniscule brain like on an overexposed film.

Perhaps someone was expecting the ant for lunch? Perhaps it was his third missed meeting of the week. Perhaps not. Perhaps the ant had all the time in the world.

It stood unmoving for some time, observing the mountain of quivering, indefinable flesh that was Migwash seated in the middle of his shelter. Then it seemed to make up its mind. It picked up a grain of sand (that it first selected with the greatest care according to criteria that, for Migwash or anyone else, might appear to be hermetic and unfounded, but that the ant, on its scale, could no doubt appreciate). After examining it from every angle, the ant shouldered it and carried it for a meter or so, then deposited it just a few centimeters from the big toe of Migwash's left foot. Meanwhile, the owner of that foot watched the scene, and his perplexity grew.

The ant paused for a moment, as if to make sure that Migwash had understood the message (or, at least, that he had understood the intent to transmit a message—that was expecting a lot from two such different species), then it went off in search of a second grain of sand—huge pebbles, actually—that it painstakingly placed beside the first one. For hours the ant came and went, so that by nightfall it had constructed a tiny sandhill—a towering pyramid—a few centimeters from the big toe of Migwash's left foot.

Darkness settled and Migwash fell asleep, as was his habit, until the following Saturday. Once the morning mists had slowly dissipated, revealing the distant volcanoes of Xerox and the wind foundries of the Gueuse, Migwash, who had slept badly, dreaming as always of military coups and suspicious alibis, noticed that the ant had not rested. Its pyramid was nearly a centimeter high, and would double its size by the time the sun reached the meridian. The ant persevered. This was something more stubborn than vocation. The ant worked fast and well. The plumbing had already been installed, the plasterers would be arriving at the end of the day and the furniture and household appliances would be delivered before the end of the week.

Migwash wanted to do something, make a contribution of his own. But the circumstances were not right. He would appear ridiculous if he tried to pick up grains of sand with his great sausage fingers. Besides, he wouldn't have known which ones to choose.

The ant, whose name may have been Eleanor, was already looking ahead to her vacation. She imagined herself on the beach. Her work done, her task accomplished. But what mattered now was to complete what she had begun. These at least were

< 77 >

Migwash's thoughts as he noticed Eleanor courageously beginning to build a second pyramid.

Migwash exclaimed, "But it's not exactly the National Holiday!" Then he immediately withdrew the impertinent remark, hoping he had not spoken it aloud. Migwash didn't want any trouble. He'd had his fill in recent years. They had their eye on him ever since the business about the unsolicited transfusions had captured the headlines at the end of the last century. Migwash recognized the ant as his equal: both were under observation. But that didn't seem to distract either from their occupations. Migwash worked at the waste disposal site. Eleanor built pyramids.

Now it was the sixth day, and the ant had begun her seventh pyramid. The geometric disposition of these seven wonders—only a few centimeters from the big toe of Migwash's left foot—suggested a fabulous ideogram. It was not yet an intelligible message, with its own content: an exposition, a development, a conclusion. But it did suggest that a message could be formulated and understood on the condition, of course, that a common code be devised.

For the moment, it was obvious how impossible that was, and would be, at least in the foreseeable future.

< 78 >

LOLA

Back then, people could barely remember the last census. It was generally accepted that North Dakota had six inhabitants. Yet a persistent rumor suggested the presence of a seventh individual whose status seemed unclear.

When a file disappeared, we always had some difficulty tracing the corresponding individual. As if the lost file was directly responsible for the disappearance of the individual concerned, but no one would risk putting forward such an interpretation.

As far as the seventh inhabitant of North Dakota was concerned, it was impossible to determine his ontological status until very recently. Actually, we could have barely tolerated the possibility that such an individual might have existed, or may still exist. Uncertainty grew, and the seventh inhabitant of North Dakota, wherever he may have been, probably never knew that at one particular point in the procedure, he narrowly avoided never having been born. I can recall a particularly troubled time during which no one wanted to hear anything about the seventh inhabitant of North Dakota, and his propensity for placing himself outside the periphery of an ill-defined border, which may have been that of North Dakota or some other territory, either unexplored or about to be effaced from the geographical maps and databases.

Hardly a word was heard about the seventh inhabitant of North Dakota for several decades. As a topic of conversation, it had been unfashionable in the better drawing rooms for even longer when, suddenly, it returned to the surface.

It was Lola.

Lola refused to admit she had hidden in the center of the world. Nobody could get anything out of her.

Her first official act in her capacity as the seventh inhabitant of North Dakota was to open a mall. (The shopping center bore her name, and its parking spaces were free at certain times of the day. Rumor has it that some ruins still survive on the outskirts of New Leipzig, and an ancient poster showing Lola in a vaguely suggestive pose may have been found alongside old Highway 94, a few kilometers from there.)

After that single public appearance, Lola asked to be transferred to Bismarck. She never obtained authorization, of course. Complications always crop up in an affair like that. Either Lola had too much experience, or not enough. It's true that experience is always harmful, one way or another. Yet another piece of data to be eliminated at the source.

According to the report, Lola Baldwin had not been seen since the year the last government was elected, which means nothing in itself, but implied that she may have had a secret to hide. (The discovery that year of a dozen corpses in the marshes of the Little Missouri, not far from Marmarth, persuaded the authorities to order an investigation into Lola's disappearance and her involvement in the closing of the mall with which her name was associated. But in the end, the investigation revealed that the bodies were those of a caravan of traders who had been ambushed. All the details can be found in the report.)

< 80 >

Danusha

On the eve of or perhaps the day after that day, the discovery of a decapitated woman on the steps of the city hall spread alarm among the population. The head lay, wild-eyed, a few meters from its body. There could be no doubt, declared the official: it was a suicide.

The bloody trail left by Danusha Baldwin suggested that the woman, overcome with absurd remorse, had dragged herself in the wrong direction.

AROJA

Since the beginning of the drought, with infinite patience, Aroja had been pulling weeds. Her forearms were covered with caked mud, her knees sunk deep into the ground, they were cut and bruised, encrusted with dried blood. She labored in the sun, lifting her knees with great difficulty, moving forward inexorably across the arid plain, but she was not really suffering. She was used to it. From time to time, by dark of night, she halted her work, but she did not dream. The cry that would arise from her throat at times like those could be heard from kilometers away. If only there was someone to hear it. Her cry, more like a groan than an appeal, did not seem to rise from the earth. It was the attempt to rekindle a memory buried from time immemorial, yet of celestial origin. As if, added several chroniclers, the earth were hollow—or full of sky, to be more exact. As if the underside of the world were alike in all respects to its surface.

But Aroja did not even consider the possibility. Nothing could have interested her less. The sun burned down. Drought ravaged the earth and she had no time to waste on such matters. As soon as it was possible, she set to work, pulling weeds. Sometimes her numbed fingers would pull up a sprout of alfalfa or clover instead of a weed. It did happen. When she realized her mistake, she displayed no sign of impatience or dismay. Quite the opposite. She exhibited exemplary solicitude, scratching at the earth with her fingernail, and delicately returning the young sprout to its place. She would even deposit a bit of her own saliva around its roots, and it was touching to see her carrying out her rescue operation, because we women all knew she was risking her life. Dear Aroja!

ITSUKO

Itsuko was no contortionist.

On rainy days, she would listen to the drumming of the water on the tin roof of her shelter. When she couldn't stand the din any more, she unfolded her knotty body and went to lie down on a rocky ledge several kilometers upstream. At times the violent currents almost carried her out to sea, where a new life awaited her. Itsuko knew that. Yet she struggled with all her strength against the hostile currents and powerful whirlpools, twisting and turning as best she could, flailing at the surface with her ridiculous little purple flippers. And she triumphed! She vanquished the current and grabbed on to whatever she could: algae, roots, rocks, the mud itself! Her new life could wait. She would go no further, she would stop holding her breath. On and on she swam. For hours, she thrashed at the water before turning back to her shelter. Once she was safe, Itsuko would breathe very hard, her hand over her heart, and she would tell herself that this could have been the end, this time. But, no, it hasn't come to that yet, not this time, not the right time.

The once and for all time.

GWENDOLYN

The Hotel Unicorn had been full for so long that the painted sign on the front window had begun to fade. A sharp-eyed observer could make out the letters NO VA and wager on the rest, but everyone knew there was nothing to be gained in that direction.

Gwendolyn started working at reception from the very beginning. The only disadvantage of the position—and she had never really gotten used to it—was the flies. There were millions of them in the hotel lobby, grounded by the torrid heat, clustered together in bunches, swarming over one another. When Gwendolyn came through the door, each of her steps would make a black cloud rise up, only to fall back a few seconds after she passed.

Flies are stubborn insects.

Gwendolyn took as few steps as possible. Most of the time she stayed behind her counter. From time to time, to keep herself in shape, she would smile at the nothingness, exactly as she would have for a customer, had one appeared. She would smile a toothsome smile and say, in the self-assured tones of the receptionist who tolerates no retort, "Terribly sorry, we have no vacancy."

At the Hotel Unicorn, aside from the buzzing of the flies, all was silent. Gwendolyn could remember the day (a day long ago) a would-be customer presented himself at the desk. He was wearing rubber hip waders, a smoky cigarette butt dangled from his lips, and he carried a fishing rod in his hand. It was her first customer, and since she had never seen one before, she imagined they all looked like him.

"Fly-fishing?"

"Yes."

"Terribly sorry, we have no vacancy."

All the same, Gwendolyn told him he could park his camper in the hotel parking lot if he wanted to. The disappointed customer wandered off in that general direction. Had he followed Gwendolyn's advice and availed himself of the parking lot? Might he even still be there?

When she imagined what a would-be customer might look like, the image of that one always came to mind. Still, Gwendolyn knew how unlikely it was that a new would-be customer, should he ever appear, would resemble the previous one, but since she had nothing to compare him with … It bothered her, having to visualize that would-be customer, with his rubber boots and fishing rod, and not another one, more athletic in appearance, or cuter. But she'd long since gotten used to the idea and no longer dared, even in her thoughts, to be unfaithful to that unique, irreplaceable would-be customer.

Some days, the pressure was immense. Conventions followed one another in rapid succession, and her workload would increase. Besides her regular hours at reception, Gwendolyn had to work in the kitchen nights and weekends. That wasn't easy. The flies multiplied relentlessly, as if they were aware of how few moments they had left, and that theirs was a race against time.

Once in a while—especially toward the end—Gwendolyn thought she heard coughing from one of the rooms. Something was moving in there, no doubt about it. The sound of snoring would sometimes rattle the walls, but that was rare. And not very reassuring. But her would-be customer would always come back. He would cross the lobby, ignoring the billions of swarming flies, come to a standstill at the desk, an old cigarette butt dangling from his lips, and Gwendolyn would flash him her sweetest smile.

"Terribly sorry, we have no vacancy."

< 85 >

SYLVIA

Black Lake must have caught fire during the night. It was lovely to see, the red glow in the distance, and exciting. It gave you a foretaste of reality, but more than that, and no one could deny it, it gave off all kinds of toxic fumes, and the banks themselves could go up in flames at any moment. Already, patches of underbrush were hissing and popping malevolently, waiting for the slightest breath of wind to spread the fire.

Sylvia Baldwin alone claimed responsibility for the attack. She had acted on her own. From then on, she was called the Sylvia Cell. All that was written in the prospectus with a photo of the yellow cat Sylvia had found.

Charges were laid, but the Sylvia Cell was not to be found. They searched the abandoned factories, the high-plains foundries, the harbors and marshaling yards, all the places Sylvia would likely go to await the end. Someone even walked the whole distance from Sainte-Flavie to Boston to hand the Wanted poster to the proper authorities. But all these combined efforts proved fruitless.

Zones J 24 and N 39 were quickly declared disaster areas. They remain so to this day, since Black Lake continues to burn. It burns on in the Arctic night as a warning to future generations. Its flame may well be eternal. From time to time, even though it's forbidden, a caravan passes nearby. Some will even make a detour, given the necessary inducement, to let the adventurous approach the gaseous column that's visible from kilometers away, and whose infernal breath can be smelled even further than that, sometimes even here, in the secondary corridors of the fourth level.

In the meantime, Sylvia found a hiding place for herself and the yellow cat. It may have been the abandoned hangar of a former military base, or an ammunition dump or a laboratory: filthy rooms with broken windows and empty, dusty shelves. There was plenty of activity here at a certain time, but that must have been long, long ago.

In a corner, Sylvia bent over the yellow cat and the kittens that were coming into the world one after another, like the tiny, blood-stained pearly beads of a rosary. The cat had been giving birth for days, and sighed each time she brought forth a yellow kitten, but she was far too weak to turn her head and lick them as she should have done.

As she felt she should have done.

Sylvia took the tiny blind things in her hands and finished the job of cleaning them. The taste was salty, but not at all unpleasant.

< 87 >

VICTOR

Victor Baldwin, that naturally disarming engineer, that most discreet of beings, may well have dug holes in the highway. Piles of holes. The only way to estimate their depth was to fall into them, but it was forbidden even to get close. So powerful was their attraction, once you came close to the edge, that you would be compelled to throw yourself down, headfirst. Life would be easy at the bottom of the prefabricated abysses. The captives would feel neither hunger nor thirst, warmth nor cold. The light would be constant at all times, and their eyelids would act as shutters when necessary. Closing them would shade the light to an emulsifying pink, but the residents would still be able to see—which meant the contemplation of their internal organs. The terms of residency provided certain visiting rights: members of the immediate family, a class of civil servants expressly appointed for that purpose, even a household pet could claim them. To be sure, caimans and vultures would enjoy extraordinary prerogatives.

We would all be quite comfortable. An infinite library to which we would never have access would be the guarantor of our innocence. Once every thousand years or so, a messiah would emerge from our group to enthral us with an illusion so lifelike that our vices would be flattered and exalted as vividly as possible.

That would be our finest recompense of all!

Amaryllis

If Master Baldwin had not existed, he would have had to be invented. No one knew how long he had held his arms outstretched toward a mute, warped sky. No one ventured any more into this vale of concrete and steel. The foundries were silent; only a few freighters lay rotting at the quays. No one dared come this way. Unless they were seekers of oblivion, or some other form of consolation from which there is no return.

No one appreciated the derelict hills, heaped one upon the other as far as the eye could see, that brought to mind an endless disposal site. They frightened tourists. They inspired in them no pity. They spoke of the pride of the Baldwins who had survived despite the slenderest of probabilities.

Until the day Amaryllis came and decided to live in his shadow.

In the shadow of Master Baldwin who, had he not existed, would have had to be invented.

That was the year the last government was elected, of course.

Amaryllis could have been anywhere else. She knew it. To be anywhere else was in her power. Even though the shaman was avaricious—and perhaps for that very reason—she had come to seek the science of a thousand worlds in the shadow of Master Baldwin. Everything was impregnated with his being. It overflowed the self. This vale of concrete and lamentations.

Amaryllis demanded answers. Through the winter, she questioned, "Why do all things revolve but us?" Or, indeed, "If there are only the two of us here, how could someone exist somewhere else? How, indeed, could any place exist outside our imagination?"

Master Baldwin simply smiled, and extended his knotty arms even higher toward the sky. He had never been in the habit of answering questions like that. And he was not about to begin now, after centuries of abstinence. The barren stones, the dark rock and the bitter hardness of the sky: all confirmed how right he had been. Though Amaryllis might blush with shame, Master Baldwin remained unmoved. The sky, the wind, the black stones and the refuse piled up here over the course of the centuries seemed to lend their tacit agreement. In the distance the horizon was frenetically breaking into fragments under a red-rust sky. The mornings were chilly, the afternoons scorching, the nights endless. The steely desert left no barrier between them and what remained of infinity.

No one knows exactly when Amaryllis gave up on finding the answers that had brought her so far from her home. The fact that she'd never received a single one somehow helped ease her anxieties. Her initial impatience had become a burden, and now she was relieved of it.

One day, Master Baldwin opened his chest and, in an unprecedented surge of altruism, pulled out his beating heart. He bent over Amaryllis and placed it in her hands. It was a diminished heart. The Master's last authentic organ. Amaryllis breathed in its essence, then she restored it as best she could to its original place.

"Well done," said the Master.

< 90 >

EPILOGUE

With regard to the preceding chronicles, we would like to emphasize that they both express and inspire a sense of legitimate dismay. Each rekindles the debate: are the Baldwins part of the conditioning process, or do they simply represent an extended form of unknowing? The College believes that a definite answer to this question will never be given, no matter how it is raised. Still, irrespective of one's point of departure, distinctions must be drawn.

According to Ganidor, the Baldwins had almost certainly, in an era that remains uncertain, domesticated the whole of the peripheral system and its virtual extensions. A small number of Baldwins may still survive, in his view, in the retransmission of some forty all but inaudible messages. How many exactly? Ganidor cannot say. In this matter, as in others, his confirmation has more in common with speculation than with scientific method. This he makes no attempt to conceal. "No one will ever convince me that such a stubborn species could have simply vanished, just like that, without leaving the slightest trace!" he writes in The Survival of the Baldwins.

Following Drigø, our eminent colleague, the Baldwins can be taken to represent an exemplar of permanent projection, or (to use an expression dear to Drigø) projections of varying duration. In a startling work published several years ago,[1] our colleague attempted to demonstrate that the Baldwins are the result of a millennium of fanaticism and internal struggle within the Permanent Bureau itself. They may well have been devised by the latter for purposes that, argues the author, remain hermetically outmoded. Indeed, it is difficult to conceive what motives could possibly have induced the

---

1. Drigø. *The Greatest Practical Joke Since the End of History.* Adrenaline Press, London, 1863.

Permanent Bureau to represent the Baldwins in such aberrant form; did they not drag themselves across the surface of a world that has always been hostile to them? Their survival seems so utterly contingent that it makes them appear undesirable! Their superfluous nature may even be described as ontological! Such are the objections that Drigø carefully refrains from raising, and one readily understands that such pointed questions leave him ill at ease.

Thus expressed, Drigø's theory appears as incoherent as it is plausible. It has remained, nonetheless, the opinion most often expressed and most accepted by the public at large for the last five peripheral centuries.

In truth, if the Baldwins appear to have adapted so easily to the horror their condition inspires, it is as a result of pure compassion for themselves and those like them. They define themselves in no other way, it seems to us, than by the unspeakable silence that continues to linger in the wake of their disappearance, in the mind-defying act of survival atop the most brilliant heights, in that princely sense of self-importance that makes them at once so foreign and yet so like us.

The Baldwins resemble us: they knew nothing of their origins, nor of their destination.

They can hardly be faulted for that.

< 94 >

Acknowledgements

The chroniclers would like to thank Linda Baldwin, Annie Baldwin, Eloi Baldwin, Jacob Baldwin, Laynya Baldwin, David Baldwin, Mathieu Baldwin, Sophie Baldwin, Olivier Baldwin, Ruth Baldwin, Gudrun Baldwin, Falstaff Baldwin, Takashi Baldwin, Basmara Baldwin, Itsuko Baldwin, Natasha Baldwin, Ben Baldwin, François Baldwin, Bevinda Baldwin, André and Andrée Baldwin, Eléonore Baldwin, Suzie Baldwin, Bruno Baldwin, Victor Baldwin, Enayat Baldwin, Gregor Baldwin, Kito Baldwin, Lee Baldwin, Amaryllis Baldwin, Desmond Baldwin, Lothar Baldwin, Jocelyne Baldwin, Max Baldwin, Otto Baldwin, Sylvia Baldwin, Sheida Baldwin, Tom Baldwin, Ogata Baldwin, Malcolm Baldwin, Magali Baldwin, Gretchen Baldwin, Lori Baldwin, Tonino Baldwin, Christophe-Benjamin Baldwin, Landrio Baldwin, Lena Baldwin, Francine Baldwin, Richard Baldwin, Hermina Baldwin, Sara Baldwin, Lola Baldwin, Nathalie Baldwin, Patrick Baldwin, Danusha Baldwin, Aroja Baldwin, Nicole Baldwin, Gabrielle Baldwin, George Baldwin, Jonathan Baldwin, Chantal Baldwin, Tasha Baldwin, Josée and Louise Baldwin, Master Baldwin and the Smoke. Thanks also to Mike Baldwin and to all the Baldwins at the end of the world, in Maisonnette and Anse Bleue.